I0529798

SOFT TSUNAMI

By the Author

Dolly: Memoirs of a High School Graduate
If You Love Me, Come

SOFT TSUNAMI

by

Claudia Moss

Soft Tsunami

© 2012 By Claudia Moss. All Rights Reserved.

ISBN 13: 978-0-9832697-1-7

This book is a collection of poetry.

First printing 2012

THIS BOOK, OR PARTS THEREOF, MAY NOT BE
REPRODUCED IN ANY FORM WITHOUT PERMISSION.

CREDITS
COVER PHOTO BY ZENPRESSIONS -- ATLANTA
COVER DESIGN BY CLAUDIA MOSS

Dedication

To every writer who ever longed to lift a pen to give voice to the songs in her soul. This is for you.

Preface
My Inner Sea

Even before I knew definitively that I'd be standing on the shore of this work, my first poetry collection, looking out on my inner sea, I knew that this day would come. It was written like Sanskrit on my Soul, splashed across wire-bound notebook sheets, trickled down yellow legal pads and, eventually, tap-danced across my laptop's lit screen, lined up and regimented like sexy showgirls awaiting applause.

Knew as I wrote myself poetic prescriptions for my sanity when life was a too-tight cocoon I wondered would ever release me…a fully armored, pen-welding nymph, writing her way into a tomorrow she cherished in dreams. Life. If it wasn't going my way, I culled a poem. If it warranted celebrating, I sketched a portrait. If it caused my knees to quake, I baked manna of iambic pentameters and free verse. In short, I saved me from the hot confines of a closet that shrank with the years, squeezing me out into the light of acceptance and the plurality of who I am. Uniquely me.

In 2011, I knew when I called my photographer friend, Zen, and requested a sensual, artistic photo shoot at high noon on Stone Mountain one chilly October morning and my beloveds, Kiyandrea and LaKenya, answered my call to assist me on the shoot and Zen ended up photographing me near warming water the older the day grew, I knew, a year later, this collection would bear a watery name: **Soft Tsunami.** Add to this I've cell memory of lifetimes beside the sea in recent incarnations I sense in the chambers of my heart.

Thus, out of the sea within, I wade to sugar-white sand on a moonlit beach…a Sapphic Siren…invited by the Universe to make a special appearance to sing the songs I sing.

TABLE OF CONTENTS

Touch

I want to touch you,
Feel you, inhale you, kiss you to
s i g h s.
My goal, to caress your soul.
You can trust this touch.
I've waited a lifetime   to wade into you.
I am your buoy in the deep, my love.

To stroke you 1,000 ways
Experience the logarithms of your heart,
Hold you to my breast,
One ravenous palm at your lower back
The other laced in your coils
Your fluttering lashes dragonflies pulsing   in my veins
Is my soul's one desire.

Though you're motionless
I can feel you tremble,
Blossoming   surging
Your petals dewy,
The air moaning
In surround undulations.
I'm grateful the Universe has answered   us.

Thus, I stroke you softer than quill skimming rice paper.
A message of calligraphy teasingly rough
Gasping at the taste of us.
Touch-tethered   we are.

Touch (revisited)

May I know you?
Touch you past the ravine of
Insecurity
That has you imprisoned
In an era that watched you undress
In a closet inside yourself
To make love in undergarments
With the lights out.
I can caress you beyond our divide,
My knowing surmising your needs
Softer than butterfly wings
Fanning you from within.
If you stilled you
Long enough to touch me back,
You would know the various terrains
Of my skin's continents.

May I touch you?
Take your hand and pull you   up
From the well of
Hand-me-down mores and
Lay-away sensibilities
Dictating what you couldn't, shouldn't, ought not to do,
Considering all they said it would lead to
Is you being felt up and
Leftover
Unworthy to be asked to an altar
They erected.

Touch Tether Twine   Tat Thread Tie Twist
Me to you
You to me.

I AM THE WIND

I am The Wind
Blowing breezes, gentle and sweet, of love and affection
Across the pages of your life. I quiver nerves, shatter misconceptions
Of what it means to be you, when you adore someone the World
Says you ought not to love romantically.

Come, I'll bow to you,
Permit you to ride me,
While I whisper what it could be
If you remembered, you are already free
To fly with me.

As free as us playing in leaves, a frolicking breeze
Dispelling phantom climaxes from times before.
We hump
Your judgments loose.
In December's crisp freshness,
Leaving you tossed, lost, then found
Like tumbleweeds racing Arizona ground.

I AM
The Wind,
And I come for You, and You, and Her, and Him, and Them
Wherever you are....in a locked mind, on the other side of policy,
trapped in a dynasty, in a virtual closet, on stage, at work, in high ranks,
under oath, across seas, next door, up under fear...

I am
The Wind.
Nothing is off limits to where I can be.
Next time I tickle your fancy,
Open the door to pleasures beyond your deepest imaginings.

i think of you...

when the winter wind whips the lawn chairs across the back porch

and the angry chimes take cymbal lessons in the twilight

and the chirping of cold crickets splices the night

under the music of Carlton's neighborly midnight blues

with the hum of the frig moving the silence

and the smell of already-eaten vegetables and russet potatoes

flavoring the kitchen's warmth with a buttery peace

and the radio spills frayed tunes

while my Lenovo's keys tap and sing

and thoughts of cuddling lulls me to snuggle chilly sheets upstairs,

i think of you...

A Minute Maid

A minute and she is swimming in my veins, thump-thumping in the back of my knees driving me insane---while my internal reservoirs stream. My blood pressure takes wings and swirls under my skin like a bevy of acupuncture stings. Under her lips, icebergs come undone, careen, and flow.

I Don't Remember You

I swear   I don't   remember you,

But my arms claim a
Different refrain, insist you
wrapped me
In the grinding sway of
A slow-moving train, panting
And jet-hued, your talking
Breath on my neck, whispering what
You can do and how,
My body attests it's true,
Your cleverness
Ingenious
In my pores
Spurring recollections of a touch
Absorbed
A touch
Marking me as yours.

Yet I assure you   I don't remember   you

Though my pink flower
In its silky bower
Gleams for hours when I'm
Subjected to its
Distraction
At the mention
Of your name
Its petals
Tight-lipped
Obedient to me
Not the incandescent

Tremor it hides
Inscribed
With the memory of
Your   moans.

I promise you I do   not   remember you

Although your daisy-chain of wet kisses,
My leg misses
Still burns and climbs the inside of
My thigh, while
Your sassiness
I've learned
Has tattooed your name
In my false flesh
Determined, I see
To make a mockery of
My steadfast certainty
That my knees, my toes,
The back of my thighs
Know not the songs
You sang and
The laugh you
Left to dance
Across my
Ass.

Truly I vow   to the last   I don't remember   you
However, my senses are winded
Staring down this dissension
Totally up-ended
Wondering **how**:
How my tastebuds can't ignore
Delight wrought from your roseate core,

How my nose refuses to flout
The lingering musk you wore,
How my ears discount not
Tantalizing tales of our magical   lore,
How the sight of you reveals
My new love a bore,
How the touch of you leaves
Me wanting   to be   explored.
L o r d!

May the Goddess decry
Who tells the lie!

Even
              Though
                            I don't
                                          Remember

                    Y

                        O

                        U

To Reach You

If I only knew how to reach you, I wouldn't need words to paint
these lines
wouldn't be standing behind this mic
clocking time
a portrait of everything these smiling lips can't seem to say
leaving me stranded on a distant shore
so far away
out of focus
wondering how others command attraction in multitudinous
frames
translating visual touch to easel
a melic brush
that softly waits to stroke passion up and down, around and
around, in and out
across silky places
I long to go
to lace
you
to me
closer than corset eyes
with traces of our love…our breath…our scents…
in my caramel colors
oiled
in these textured curves
and
penciled warmth.
See…
if I knew how to
have you
I wouldn't walk in and not speak,
not make eye contact,
not wanting to see rejection in your

swagger,
wouldn't take half the night to bow to
a magnetism
as strong as tides
so I let you slide
holding out to only end up beside
you
speechless
though
in my mind
I tell myself this and that, reasoning
empty
no rabbit in the hat, and when you walk
away
not knowing
you star
in my dreams
it's okay.
Buoyant
I close the door
again
'cause
next time
I'll know
how to
sculpt
everything
my heart holds
and not give a gotdamn
if you
stay or go.

I Want a Lyrical Lady

To woo me, you don't have to be a many splendid thing
Have a trove of riches in trust or mutual funds to warrant my time
There are ladies more attuned to those manufactured, prefabricated
lines
Simply, I've found...they just don't make my heart sing.

I love diamonds as much as the next sister, but the bling
Corresponds with other characteristics that need be present
For the gift of my time, as I'm not a gold digger and her ring
Will never be accepted if she knows not how to mine the gold in my
mind.

The Goddess knows great sex is something that must be addressed
Two as one in sensual caress is undoubtedly blessed,
Yet my body, my limbs, my erogenous zones
Follow my cerebral, my need to be lyrically entranced to be undressed
My climax titillated, stroked and honed
On the lips of a Lyrical Lady
Who owns my moans, my soul, my heat with the sensuality she
Metes
In the way she leads me mentally
To our boudoir of poetry.

Only she welds the poetic prowess to strip me
Make me climb the pole of her dic...tion
Stanza by stanza
Leaving me perennially high, sweating and won,
Elation engulfing me in unadulterated bliss
As she spits the rhythmical gist of why and how she adores me
Croons softly of the future she can see of us
If I am present enough
To feel her penetrate my soul with rhapsodic melodic intent.
For her, I'm bent
In any position that renders her content.

I want a Lyrical Lady
Whose lyricism leaves me shivering in the wake of the profound
In the way she puts it down

A lyricist
In whose hand a pen croons instead of demands
A lady unafraid to lyricize about loving and being loved
Unafraid of being touched without the touch-me-not duress
Of some too afraid our togetherness, woman-to-woman
Might remind her of what she binds, hides, contrives to disguise.

O tis true, I want a Lyrical Lady
You keep the looker and the shady
Give me **that** one
Gifted and skilled in the melodious will to unabashedly
Take me, command me, hypnotize me
With expressive thoughts and charismatic feelings
The one whose kisses leaves me reeling
Under the pithy comforter of her free verse, sonnets, raps, limericks,
haikus, songs and odes.

Oooh yeees!
Give me
A
Lyyyrrricaaal
LADEE

For You, I Will

My Star Stud
My Beautiful Butch

> My Bold Bulldagger
> My Boi Toy

I Will

> Dance nude on a Fiji beach in moonlight
> Make the sun rise throughout the night
>
> Shower you in a love supreme
> From your throat bring a million screams
>
> Leave you on your back for hours on my bed
> My tongue so divine, you'll lose your head.

For Me

> Your Fabulous Fem
> Your Lipstick Lesbian
> Your Darling Dyke

You always

> Light my fires one by one
> Then put them out slow and easy just for fun
>
> Kiss me 'til my curls are wet with sweat
> Then hold me till the fight is won
>
> Compose lyrics to songs unsung

Rock me to the rhythm of the Rising Sun.

For You

Are the words.
I am the page.

I am the melody,
You the percussion.

I am the rage,
You the revelation.

I Will

Choose you forever.
You are my passion.

I am your tempo.
You are my beat.

I am the moment.
You are my finest hour.

A Minute

She only had a minute. Within 60 seconds, she knew she had to win it. Got me to sing her fame in a loud chorus, like I'd never loved until I screamed her name and script her notoriety in the stars from Venus to Mars. Just a look, a wink, a smile, I think, and her minute held our eternity in it.

Beloved

like beloved, i'm pregnant
        with the desire to love you
        to be your love

i want to engorge myself
        with the salty taste of your ocean
        no cares to what others might say

standing naked, i hide nothing
        from your inquisitions about my past
        from your acquisitions of my present

see, my eyes gulp you greedily, framing details
        to mount you in the front room of my soul
        like diamonds in Sethe's ears

unlike beloved, though, i don't plan to vanish in my tracks
        'cause i'm gone wait you out, walk you down,
        be the stars in your crown

no, i ain't going home, back to Spirit, without loving you, again

I Lose My Mind

At the sight of you
Don't understand
Though it seem simple
Like one and one make two

You send me
In the lines of old-school songs

You wet me
In places I ain't been, didn't know was there

You lead me
To the edge of the world

You silence me
Voice snatched like a star-stuck girl

I lose my mind
Under the heat of your stare
Don't understand
Guess some things God don't want shared

I done quit calculatin'
Never was good at long division
Just tryin' not to lose the rest of me
Now you know the power you weldin'

Don't seem fair
You don't 'pear to lose nothing
When you see me lost
And I done learned the cost
Of yo' touch when you reach out

Yo' hand and ask me where I'm goin'
Where I wanna be
Like I got sense enough to
Look out for me

And like that---
The ground buckle
Got me wobblin' like a newborn deer
Wind rise up suddenly---
I cain't hear
Can only grab hold
Do what the resta my mind
What don't run off
Know to do when you near
Like Janie Crawford
I watch the sky
And feel what it feel like
To love
When yo' mind done got up and gone
Bye bye

You Want Me

Though you don't know it yet
But, Gyrlfriend,
Please believe
It's a bet

I'm the one
Who'll leave you wet

Don't care
If you never admit it

I told ya
I'll be your self-help guide
Leave you beguiled

Have you getting up off
Your knees
In your attempt
To please
Me

Are you shy?

Are your lips
As soft as your eyes?

Hold my hand
And I'll

Make you do things
You only thought
Made the others cry

Don't you know I'd die
To put it down so fie
You be my junkie
Hounding me
For the next fix
Whipped---
Your eye on the prize
Between my thighs

Baby

You really want me
So don't fight the feeling
Dealing
Like I didn't warn you

I got you
Entwined

As tight
As the plump curls
In your locs

Your thoughts on hoc
Locked
Down
As
Flat
As
Your back
On my
Mattress

Don't play, Babee,

Stay
It's wicked
I know
But if you
Stick it
Just right
Tonight
I'll remix
The tension in your temples
My trademark
Left
In your
Skin
To broadcast
Memories
Next time you
Pretend
You
Don't
Want
Me

Why you wanna clown?

Be too late
You wait
And

I will write
You
Outta my
Secret places

Flat unlace you

Forget you made
My heart
My pulse
Vie in races

So don't try me,
Lady

Denial

i knew
she was
wifed up
the way
she coughed
my name.

did it
like she
hugged up
with fear.

too bad
i'm too
loved up
to move
on the
DL,
my dear.

Haiku

didn't you promise to
answer when i called, if i
needed you, my love?

Haiku No. 2

no, thanks. i'll take mine
straight, no lipstick, please, only
mine on her will do.

Haiku No. 3

if i could, i'd flush
u out of my heart like i
didn't give a good shit.

Haiku No. 4

forget my heart, my
purse empty and this affair
just got old, baby.

I Can't Explain

Why I bowed to your stone wall the night we met
And you refused to be dismissed
By my ill-mannered etiquette
At your nerve, your non-stop verse
Of what we could do, just me and you
Talkin' 'bout you loved a fem with muscular arms
And fierce-tongued charm

I can't explain
What made me spend the night in the parking lot
After the venue was locked and folks left
No one to see or hear the smooth moves you used   you were
so hot
Drawing me into stories of your growing up, teen years and
coming out
O woman, you worked my ears
Without a doubt
But I stayed, didn't miss a word, even after the Moon
Dimmed her front-porch light

I really can't explain
Jeopardizin' a brawl not comin' home and all
Lounging with you on that upstairs sofa
Laughing as your plumed ghetto bird cut the fool and watching
the Tube
Knowing I didn't want to be caught tipping in after midnight
The next morning trailing me, an illicit shadow
Wondering why it took me hours to get up and go:
I didn't belong to you
Nor you me, both of us with mates out on dates
Biding time, no notions of decisiveness

Really, Love, I can't explain
Cherishing those late-night calls replete with sweet
Absolute nothings and passed-around conversations
You sharing my intellect
With anyone who could recollect
The splendiferous delight
Of chatting with a mango-voiced woman in the middle of the
night

Guess I'll never explain
Why we didn't make love
Though I'm positive I loved you
Ms. Fear, that ole Lingering Lady, nudged her way between us
While we cuddled in lust:
You terrified of where I'd been
Me petrified of where I was going
Both of us knowing
We were already the sweetest of memories
Lo siento, pero no puedo explicar.   Really…I can't explain
And although such things I knew viscerally
I could no longer deign
Myself another story in your anthology
Our mythology
Glorious yet sordid
Cherished and abused
So I walked away not to lose
Myself
After the glory
Of loving you
Shifted
Gifted
Me with the grace
To release
You

A Wedding Poem: "Rhapsody in Blue"

She is
A rhapsody
In melodies as ancient and elegant as
Free-flowing poetry
An epic poem
My Nubian composition
She speaks to me in tones of love
In meters of passionate verse
Unrehearsed
With modulated tenderness
Others bow to
Wondering how we two
Share a current so rare
So true
You see, I recite her
And she---
She interprets me.

She is my musical muse
Embracing my irregularities
Accepting me for me
Desire sublime in her eyes
In her heated touch
When, under her prowess, she plays
Me

In notes
Creating an improvisational masterpiece
As she adores me, watching while
I scat up and down the scales
Of her artistry

Open as I am to whatEVER
She desires of me.
I don't mind if you know that
She is my enthusiastic talk
I spill wherever I am:
In the choir
At play
Up in your Mama's living room
No matter
My lips part
And my heart races forth
To sing the magic of our intrigue.

When she writes
I am her exalted novella
Written in loving chapters that
Undress our rawness
A translation
I lie bare atop her fiery sheets
In Seventh Heaven,
Alert, alive, and attentive
Her "Rapsodia"
Willing to communicate in languages
I don't speak
Just to know again the beauty she is:
The cool skin, the suppleness of her hair
The satin lips, the pulse under her flesh
The intellect draped in wit
In the gift of her Presence
My Thesaurus pales and wails
Fighting to offer adjectives
To say: "That is it! This is how we fit!"

Yes, she is my ecstasy

And, yes, I am her bliss
Thus today, on a glorious Saturday morning in June,
She is my bride
And I---well
I am her wife, an ever-present delight in the rest of her life.

for Amelia and Lorene

Ah, She Needs Be A Memory...

It would save her heart, that's for sure.
I'd not have to do her
And leave my leftover kisses to lure
The next unfortunate Miss to drink of my liquor.
       I would not care if she fed me grapes.
       I'd leave her standing at my front gate.

Her car I would confiscate.
Her finest friend I would surely date.
O she needs be a memory,
If she dare thinks of playing games with me.
       On her celly, I'd use two thousand, prime-time
       minutes.
       Then I'd pay her to, with anger, dial my digits.

Without protest, she'd pay my car note and my rent.
For Christmas, she'd buy and buy me until she's spent.
And if I heard tell she lied
I'd dismiss her before the next sunrise.
       I might offer classes in "How to Make a Heffa Holler."
       Fems would come from near and far with stiff dollars.

I defy the vows she professes to live by.
I'd flip her and leave her wondering why.
The word "fishy" she'd embrace,
And drape it about her shoulders like Spanish lace.
       Ah, Madam will want **me** to be a memory.
       From me, she'd unwrap the sweetest misery.

Cultivation

If I grew under ATL sun
And watched my vines run
Peachtree-named streets,
Would you water my roots
As liberally
As you prune Janelle vines
That race the lattice of
Your roof?

Fem Dreams

Hey, Boo
Yes, you,
with the perfect mix of boy in yo' gyrl
no frills, no curls,
You

Lend me your Being
for right Now
Listen with your heart, not your mind

I won't settle for less
my request your total presence
at best

Get it?

The past and future aside
look into my eyes
Tell me no lies

If you dwell in Truth
and She in you
you know it's nothing new

The right Fem touches the deepest part of you
straight leaves you confused

Your emotions you hope she doesn't abuse
seeing she's got your head in a flurry
you hurry
to see her stiletto stroll
into a room
tip toeing your pulse to panic mode

that heart on boom
especially if you know
she knows
no debates
the effect of the seismic flutters
on your heartscape

Your power of speech failed
the last time she
sashayed
through your fantasy
high steppin' and prissy
she dripping through your wet dreams
forming puddles in your consciousness
her reflection
lying delicious atop your sheets
sweetness everywhere
The scene complete, it

got you stuck
on repeat

'Cause you don't know what to kiss first
her smooth sexy feet
those cheeks, Oooo those cheeks
have you humming stupid yummy tunes
about her tight crescent moons
dipped in a sepia glaze
her waist flat lining towards her cute kitty
unthonged
you'll be crazy if you can't get a quick taste
your tongue sprung
practically hurting
to be slurping her
Damn Fem about to crack your plate

Now you craving that—

Here…take the pen
you
fill it in
from start to finish
Just know she sugary
throwing you in a diabetic haze
trying to recollect if ever there were days
you said you'd never find pleasure
kissing whatever---

Here's the real deal
every molecular inch of you
seeks
her body heat
Big Gryl, quit it--   admit it--
that Fem got you beat

But you poetically cool
a right proper butch
your bag near to take Miz Fem to school
let her know whose rules she's abiding
while she's eyeing you
buckling up
tantalizing her with your tool
locked in place
a pat to its base
You betta know it…
No limp noodle can
keep your Fem
on ooze

No need for shame
you got game
you remind yourself
'cause
here she cums
the afterglow of her climax

thick on her trembling limbs
those sexy lashes flickering
eyes rolled back
you got her stuttering
that appetizing mouth muttering
your name

And her pussy whines so pretty, it stops Time
How about that?
Like a larger-than-life image on the big screen
at the Imax

And she can send it back
nothing shady
about this Fem

Now she can get it, Lady

Natural curls spill across your neck and
her hot kisses bless
the skin you're in
kicking up a furor in your chest
and then tat-kiss that stomach
where it
damn it---
parts those
thighs

And you can't remember the last time
you felt the power of the
Sublime
in the Now
your mind like HOW can this Fem
be wiping out your memory bases
fucking up traces of the last baby gyrl who
rocked your world
But you too cool, nobody's fool to let go that quickly
even when the shakes

can't be faked

Until those heart-shaped lips
head south
fire in her mouth
kisses freezing your joints like the ice in her hood
on her way to your "Head Lady in Charge"
who knows when to bow
down
under the temperature of the right Fem's lick
The flicks her tongue gives your clit
got you—
S   H   I   T!
holding sheets
head thrown back, pretense ended
eyelids suspended
holding
falling
cussing
clinging
calling her, let's say
tonight
hoping
praying
the number's right
'cause
Fem dreams alright
but
you can't wake
to another day

without

that Fabulous Fem Fantasy

by your side
in her place

Get to This...

I evict myself from your embrace
a place
that choked my breath
made me wrestle
back pent against the floor
my affections scattered
at the door
like rubble on the curb
abandoned
waiting for others
to rummage

I'm not needy
and hardly greedy
so wrap those arms
about some other Lady
accustomed to
breaking strangleholds
and decoding
padlocked heartaches

I scribble my name across the check
that cancels
any investment
linking me to you,
Boo
Get to this...
I've learned
all mutual funds
don't always yield
the potential
the fine print mentioned
Hey,
before the ink dries
I'll be vested in me finally

I hand myself a pink slip
to Freedom
just beyond my cleared desk
where I've arrested
your corporate foolishness
and tossed it
in the trash
to sit atop
other
broken promises
disillusionment
and pieces of glass
that cut my yearning
to take this love
to another ceiling

O no, my sweet,
I don't do
Head-on collisions   long
With walled feelings
Wearing Stacy Adams
And sexy boxers
Leaving me
Limp on the ropes
Of revelry
Hoping for Round Three
No, love, not me
Bruised brains ain't
My cup of tea

Get to this…
Lose my number
I signed this restraining order
And yo mama's paperweight is on the corner
Where I left the rest of your confusion
In organized parts---   So go---   And---
Be blessed, My Lady of the Broken Hearts…

I Want to Be Your Recipe

I want to be your recipe whenever you cookin'.

When you gather flour, eggs and butter,
Milk, oil and baking soda to stir into batter,
I can be the sugah to make your batter matter.

I want to be your recipe
When you stir fry.
I'll be the onions to make you cry,
Then you can caramelize me
To add the sweet and sour to your veggie melody.

I want to be your recipe
When you bake your dinner bread.
I'll be so still you can mold me, knead me,
And jelly roll me
Into something delicious enough to take to bed.

I want to be your recipe
When you slice apples for your pie.
I'll be the spice to lay across the top.
I'll be the oozing hot, bubbly brown syrup.
I'll even be the cool whip dollop
To make your taste buds hollah.

I want to be your recipe
When you're blue and tired of low-fat dishes.
I'll be your skillet of feel-good wishes.
Full of fat and carbohydrates,
I'll have you zonin'
Faster than your brain's release of serotonin.

I want to be your recipe
When you spread your pizza dough.
You can toss me up and twirl me,
Make me dizzy,
Say, "I-I can't take anymore!"
But I'll wait patiently for your pepperoni and cheese,
Then cover you in my spicy sauce,
Make YOU whisper, "Pleeeze!"

I want to be your recipe
When you boil your collards.
I'll be your hambone,
My flava creepin' through your pot,
Make you leave canned greens alone.
'Cause I'll straight terrorize your cornbread,
And make your lips my own.

I want to be your recipe
When you grill your steak.
I'll be your tenderizer,
Make you shiver and shake,
Shout, sizzle and sputter,
Rime and sign a thousand ways,
I can be your lover.

Cook me into your soul's casserole.

I Saw A Sistuh Today

I saw a sistuh today and she looked like me
and me her as she headed into a labyrinth of offices
I'd minutes vacated
notebook and pen in tow
like sistuh
who strolled towards me with notebook tucked under her arm,
armed with pen and two-stranded twists
freein' her crownin' glory from heated teeth and creamed do's
and all those natural naps boomerangin' liberated in the
afternoon breeze
like my mirror-imaged reflection.
And I wanted to shout,
"Sistuh, I likes yo style!"
But my abruptly halted parlance with a bemused colleague
told her jus' the same
'cause I didn't want her wastin' steps in a wrong direction.
And she thanked me
and what we left in a sustained smile hollered,
"Sistuh, who looks like me, you celebrated in my eyes
for embracin' what they said should be forever lost under
heat and lye and shame and style."

Today I saw me.

I Feel a Poem Coming On...

I feel a poem coming on...
when I see you standing there
calling me, beckoning me, reminding me
that I haven't been with you in a while.

I feel a poem coming on...
when you preoccupy my waking moments and
lay down beside me in the calm of the dark
to whisper how much you need me to create you.

I feel a poem coming on...
each time you flee my desperate grasp
when I feel I am ready to touch and stroke and neutralize
the foreignness that is an outcropping of our separation.

I feel a poem coming on...
when you ultimately allow me to claim you
and give birth to your poetic features
so that I know we are whole once again.

For My Next Lover, Inviting Me to Conversation

She is beside you, like sentry, when you pull up
my chair, ask me to sit for drinks in coffeeshop air

that wafts of other lives and bread and "This is why we're
here." Though your gaze strokes the slight chill from my cheek

backhanded by Atlanta's downtown wrath, she is the wraith on
your right hand, smothering our sparking embers, waiting

perchance to vent what went so terribly wrong, the reason you sit
in this place sans her golden breast poised on your arm.

How long was your last relationship? you lead eloquently, and I arch
my back and lift my breasts, and my superlative chin, and

breathe a cleansing breath before I chance how much is enough
and weigh what not to portray. In that space, in that pause, she

nudges you into a well. I watch you fade and fall, bump your
intent on the used to be, drown in the river of Forget. *Can we say*

you haven't released her yet? Then I listen as you extol the cons of
Why you left...but... she was a cruise ship on high seas, an

explorer of Caribbean mysteries, her decks aplomb with healing
oceanic breeze. She spread herself across the palate of your
appetite even after your fights tossed you out of doors and her
onto her other lover's bedroom floor. She was beauty incarnate,

with mannish ways and soft thighs, how could you not be
beguiled though her promises were dead and empty notes you

banked as though the return would come one day if you prayed
for interest instead of rain. O she, the Mother Supreme, opened

your home to family, friends, and foe indiscriminately. So you
weren't surprised the morning you found her ex's belongings

sprawled about the back bedroom, serving tray on the chenille
spread festooned with roses and leftover sunny-side up eggs and

coffee and the tattle-tell scent of her kisses on cloth napkins.
She was a red ribbon of a road winding into your past. She was

uncapped gin and sin, her sparkle left you marooned, but you
couldn't stay. I reflect, examine, say, *Babee,*

sometimes the sweetest love affair need never leave the mind.
Thank you for our meal, the conversation, and your time. I've so

many other potential lovers to interview. Then I smile my prettiest
smile, advise you to reconcile with the smug

woman by your side and walk away, knowing the reasons I
couldn't stay. I live in the moment, you the past. At this
juncture, I choose to pass. Our love need not be arrested before
its p r e d i c t a b l e impasse.

Will You Ever Leave

When I watch you walk away
When I shred albums of our yesterday
When I give away the things you left
When I block your number to give the phone a rest,

Your voice remains.

When I change my IM handle
When I clip the wick of your favorite candle
When I tell your friends you were the lover from hell
When I gather your leftovers for Saturday's yard sale,

I can yet hear your name.

When I paint my lips and strap my heels
When I flirt and grin, going in for the kill
When I scribble my number and whisper, "Take care"
When I coo into another ear, a new heart to bare,

You speak my name.

And though I slam the door against the sound

I can hear it in the iridescent bubbles rising from my bath,
Tingly laughter tickles the hairs on the back of my neck
After it scuba dives below the scented, milky froth

To wreak havoc in my underwater loft.
I can hear it between the pillows on my bed
Skipping and skating the satin like a dancer on ice
The cool music of your skates orchestrates
A symphony of blue kisses that leaves me prostrate.

I can hear it in the moans of the blues singer's guitar

In the back of the one-room joint beside the four-lane road
Where Georgia rain taps an engaging melody
In your veins and on the tin roof of my soul.

To drown the sound, I send the window crashing down.

But I can hear your whispers on midnight wind
That charms my front door, sweet-talking its way in
Just to sigh turmoil into my soul
Deafen my hearing and leave my new love cold.

I board myself against your memory
Nail you outside and throw away the key
Even caulk the cracks,
Then I peep through the foyer windows and wonder…

Will you ever leave   to come back?

Backwoods Woman: A Blues Song

I got a backwoods woman,
Way back up in the Georgia hills.
I say I got a backwoods woman, a backwoods woman,
Way back up in the Georgia hills.
She got my nose so wide open
When I leave her, my feet be standing still.
Yeah, my backwoods woman
Sho nuf
Got her mark on me
Lord, when I'm not with her
That ole love mo'jo just won't let me be.

I say I gotta backwoods woman,
Tall and fine as a Georgia pine.
Yes, ma'am, I got a backwoods woman, a backwoods woman,
Taller and finer than Georgia pines.
She keep me in lovin' so sweet
If she ever leaves, I'm certain to lose my mind.

That backwoods woman
Got lips and a tongue
As potent as moonshine
She put them on me
Lord, every moment I'm with her, be divine.

I got a backwoods woman,
A backwoods woman
Who fills my stomach and warms my bed.
O mercy, I gotta backwoods woman,
A backwoods woman
Who can serve a wet dream and turn a hose on a dry bed.
She take up with another lovah

My soul be blue and my whole world filled with dread.
Yeah, my backwoods woman
Sho nuf
Got her mark on me
Lord, when I'm not with her
That ole love mo'jo just won't let me be.

I got me a backwoods woman,
With a mind that's all her own.
Ya'll don't hear me? I said I gotta backwoods woman
Her mind is as strong as stubborn steel
She say the word
And I do her bidding with a one-track will.

That backwoods woman
Got lips and a tongue
As potent as moonshine
She put them on me
Lord, every moment I'm with her, be divine.

Yes, people, I love a backwoods woman,
Who loves harder than frost on blackberry days.
Have mercy, ya'll! I'm in love with a backwoods woman,
To cross her be worse than jail on a summer day.
My good time and halleluiah, she
Makes me so weak all I do is let her have her way.

Yeah, my backwoods woman
Sho nuf
Got her mark on me
Lord, when I'm not with her
That ole love mo'jo just won't let me be.

Could It Be a New Dis...ease?

I welcomed the morning feeling fine.
I raised the windows and parted the blinds
Only to discover by jarred surprise,
I was afflicted with heterophobic eyes.

I wondered, staring recklessly,
Mercy, could it be a new dis...ease?
If so, and this I knew for sure,
I'd be the one to invent the cure.

But imagine my horror. Imagine my shock.
There I stood watching Josie Moore lip lock.
Who cares, I thought, if Mr. Moore's off to work.
I wanted to vomit, peeping her kiss that jerk.

Head spinning, I needed flapping. Like a rug.
In Piedmont Park, I sat in sizzling sun to squash that bug.
Yet everywhere I sprinkled a smile,
Some Jane was glued to a Dick's side. Like it was all the style.

Waves of nausea caught me off guard
And sent me in search of a port-a-potty, running hard.
That ole dis...ease suddenly rose up and backhanded me,
For staring, it seemed, at such nasty scenes so publicly.

I didn't know how much more of this nonsense I could take
Until my daughter came for dinner with her new friend and a
cake. "Mama," she cooed, "Shorty asked me to marry him in
June." Not before I institutionalize you, I thought, and not a day
too soon.

Goodness, I couldn't imagine what my neighbors would say.
That girl was talking crazy, swearing she'd marry the boy anyway,

Claiming, "Ostracized? I got no worries about today or
tomorrow. "I know myself, and, Mama, our love can withstand
any sorrow."

Humph! The insanity was too much for this Suzie.
Off I went to catch a matinee movie.
Three flicks later, I'd seen enough straight scenes
To leave me feeling good and mean.

Then came the capstone of my topsy-turvy day.
My best friend called, announcing like it was okay,
Something wild just took place
When she shivered with love, looking in my Cousin Herman's
face.

That was it! "Get outta my sight!" I yelled. "Chile, please keep
that in the closet! "Let him pay the bills, even write you in his
will. Nobody has to know. "Haven't you learned how to love on
the down low?"

Then, in a flash, I developed a rash.
My body itched, limbs quivered. Hell, my whole system crashed
And left me under the bed. A sneaky snake, that dis…ease had
my eyes tearing and red.

I refuse to live like this, I said aloud.
Crawling to an open window, I bellowed to the neighborhood
crowd, "The Divine is my witness, I speak the Word.
This day forth, I choose to love everyone. There. Now y'all done
heard."

The next morning, I opened my eyes
Greeted the day and praised the sea-blue skies.
Whoever loved whomever, I judged them not
Dis…eased no more, I'm living and loving. Hate? I choose to let it rot.

Curiosity

"What type of woman
could possibly
make you feel like *that?*" she demands,
dreamy,
sinking into the sofa
dripping lust,
her lengthy dissertation
on the type of men she loves
between   us
like a

                    jade river

                                        she imagines
I can never
wade.

"The type of woman?"
I repeat,
going misty and soft with
the verdant thought of
women,
like potted tendrils
creeping over the rim
of my vase,
planting themselves
in my coils,
and blossoming
into whispers
that prune
the sprouts of her
misogyny.

I grab the sofa

To remain latticed in
The soil of such
leafy possibilities.

"The type of woman,"
I reply,
"who stands up in
an August Wilson quote
and 'makes a grand
impression
in the unmarked place.'

"The type of woman
who would rather
hang her clothes
on the flagpole
than sweat in the
closet.

"Only the sort of
woman
who is the eye
of the hurricane
and the fury
of its rain
when she perceives
a threat
to her domain."

"Oh, you're
insane,"
she chides,
adding,
"all jokes aside,

I'm curious so
keep it plain."
I give her a fertile smile,
wonder if she can
stay a while,
and continue,

"I want the
proud-to-be-gay,
wouldn't-have-it
any-other-way woman.

Give me the kind
who can wear lipstick
and combat boots

hang out with your boy
plus the one
who'll wear your skirt

talk politics till you hurt
for want of an original
conjecture

don a "Hollah Black" tee
amongst office society
knows that my wardrobe
and vanity are
off-limits,

and if she were my size
she wouldn't think of wearing my clothes
nor, with the same brush, stroke her eyes

I love a woman with few surprises,
nor guesswork in decoding
who she is, 'cause she knows
I'm the rhythm in her heartbeats
the balm on her woes,
the pussy that melts in her mouth and swallows her hand.

"O shush," she yawns, "Nobody
asked you all *that*."

Stilettos

When I don stilettos,
She lets go
Of every memory
Of every fem she's
Ever known
Ever wanted to know
Ever dreamed about…

It's a quandary
I've stopped trying
To figure out.
The things
These shoes
Can do,
Boo,
Will make a false Dom
True.

Hoe heels
Come-fuck-me pumps,
Whatever you call them---they deliver the Humph!
On command, they
Bring-her-down-a-peg
Make her beg
Wed
And
Desire to be put to bed
With sculpted legs in stilettos
Dancing in her head…
In my stilettos,
I'm Super Fem,
Able to scratch cheatin' chicks out

Without leaving the house.
I send them hell
Without breaking a nail.
And I fan them away
With my gyrl's Bitch-Be-Gone Spray.
Baby, I tell you, these shoes
Don't play!

When I don these stilettos,
My Good Gyrl is dissed
And never missed,
With her
Uncrossed knees
Throbbing like a hive of bees
At her Beautiful Butch's entry.

But in
These
Stilettos,
In my
Fem-dom,
My Butch
Cums
When I tap my feet
And strut
My stuff,
The Bad Babee in me
Softly ruff…
Pussy pumps---
That's what they are.
But they'd be the Cadillac
If they were cars.
They'd be the Big Dipper
If they were stars.

They'd be water
On Mars.
They'd be expensive Hennessey
If they were served in bars.
They'd be etched in gold
If they were excavated Egyptian jars.
They'd even be Lenin
If they were Czars...

But don't take my word:

Slip on a pair
And see how many appreciative stares they hook.
Before too long,
You'll be booked.

Caught in the black lace of your
Garter,
Dom tongues will be tattooing your slick, shiny leather.
They'll be good and reeled before they realize
You caught them
With those damn sexy, sensual, sophisticated, sassy
Fuckin' heels...

I Love You Like…

a hot shower in the middle of the night
after i've kissed a trail of fire down your belly and the sight
of you naked fills me with delight.

like a December thundershower pelting a hypnotic melody
against my kitchen's windowpane, while you, my Penelope,
accept no other lover. only for me, you wait patiently.

like a desire that dictates you want no other
almost akin to the same intense love a baby loves its mother
when just the smell of her flesh is better than a cover.

like lovin' you fills me to the seams, poppin' my stitches,
but i don't care if my britches
drag in the ditches, 'cause for your love i'd walk down witches.

like, oh yeah, grabbing a bullhorn
showing um even if this love they scorn,
i'll not be afraid to face fear and be reborn.

like the smell of freshly baked bread
that suffuses me when I sit between your legs, red
and aflame with a passion that, in some, evokes dread.

i love you like…like…i love the mango taste of your lips
in the morning when you pull on those baggy jeans and i lisp,
your beauty hard and soft at once, putting a switch in my hips.

yes, i love you like all this…

Illegal Alien

You crossed my border
Knowing you
Had no papers
On my heart
That you
Trounced
Like you knew the way through
My southern woodland

I Looked Up

And there she was
Preening in a locker-room mirror
Like the revelation of
Those copper-colored curls about
Her pixy face
And the smooth caramel
Complexion
Minus make-up
Wasn't shakin' up the whole damn place.

And that fan-yourself-quick
Body in the mirror
Sculpted to the tune of
Mo' betta blues
Cain't do right for thinkin' wrong
How many years was I born
Before you pulled up on yo' mama's good sofa
Shocked her
With the same force it
Shocked me.

I can't believe how fast I think
When such perfection strolls
Within arm's reach.

"Gyrl, you got it goin' ON
Whatchu tryin' to do—
Hurt everybody upstairs
And leave them blind, too?"
She grinned
Out of a face recently flown in
From Brazil and

Shook those curls
That, close-up, were
Naturally hers
And
Grinned again.

That close
Her lines and curves
And swerves
Required hazard signs and yields and stops and
Self-defense courses for
Heart health.

"Gone now," I teased, her
grin infectious, "'fore
You make me mad."

She broke up then,
disappeared around the corner
leaving me to fluff my 'Fro alone
in the bathroom mirror.

I looked up
From slathering buttered lotion
On my legs to make
The loud hair lay down
And there she was   again,
Grinning
Saying, "Not ready yet!
We giggled
In the same lake, the mirror
Where our faces
Spoke of different continents
Religions

Same hues
Different generations
And dissimilar milieus
But that didn't stop us from
Sharing
Our girlish moment.

Then around another corner she
Vanished
And I climbed the gym's
Basement stairs
And high jacked
An unoccupied treadmill

Just to look up
Not twenty minutes into the
Routine to shake
My own black, lightly peppering 'Fro
At her grin
And our giggles floated across
Demarcations
And machines
And we tickle ourselves anew at everyone
Watching her
Watching me
Watching us
Flirting.

Re-creation

I am a woman alone,
not lonely.
I envisioned my present while seemingly trapped
years back in another lifetime.
In the past, I walked alone, on the periphery
of a family who knocked before they entered.
I shared myself
when I wasn't
ensconced in a bedroom writing my life into the pages
I currently live.

Somebody once said,
"Recreate yourself every five years."
I vow to rewrite myself every two.

I come home to myself now.
No more the wife, the daughter-in-law---
Those parts will come again
though I will forever be a mother and now *una abuelita.*
When I think of them, I am inflated with love.
Taught my son to hold fast to his joy, to
not allow anyone
to divorce him from himself.
Tender-hearted, sometimes I bow to tongues sharpened on the
cutting board, but I am my unguent, my Band-Aid against the
lacerating wounds of the mouth, when I remember I AM.
Today I live the lessons I teach.
I am untamed, free.
I do what I want to do, say what I want to say, indiscriminately.

I am a dancer.
My feet crave bliss in clear plastic heels.

When I dance
My essence rides the clouds bareback on rainbow wings,
honoring all that I see.
You know my style beguiles you because
I dance at my ordinance.
I am my own salve. I stroke the ointment of my kisses along
my soft flesh and the cream of my juices heal, comfort, bless.

I make love to books.
Their chapters are my lovers, stimulant and vocal.
They whet my palate for passion, intellect, adventure.
I woo them while I clean   cook   cavort.
They find themselves in the creases of my sheets.
When I tire of them, I slip into a movie, meditation,
or disappear in music that saves me in stretched limbs and
leaping feet
and undulating middle and empty mind and firm behind.
Time no longer dictates the routine.
I dance because I am.

I adore myself.
I am metamorphic.
I have become the me I've seen in dreams.
My coils are a skein of self-acceptance.
In their naps, I saw the thought: Embrace your own beauty,
minus curling irons, hot combs, beveling irons hanging from the
tree of memory like heated ornaments.
Spare me a beauty on a marquee I choose not to reach.
You do you, I'll do me, eloquently.
I veil and drape sometimes.
The merchant at the Somali store sold me my first hijab.
White and lacy, it whisked me to a time I was queen.
It draped my glory and even my shoulders when I went before
the Divine.

I drape myself in yards of communicative cloth from head to toe.
Colorfully wispy saris
Speak of sensuality, without zippers and clasps, in pleats and
tucks.
I button nothing.
My belly is supple, flat, unhooked.
Cloth lies across my arm like a prayer, across my shoulder like a
firstborn.
In my full regalia, traffic ceases, talk sheared like shorn seams.

I am a dreamer.
My world springs up animatedly round about me.
I dream myself loving my soul mate infinitely, beyond the galaxy.
Hand in hand, we stroll hot, tropic sand.
I recreate myself in the peace of this thought:
What I do, I do for love.
I am a rough copy; I am a completed draft.
I am the promise of tomorrow's climax.
Recursive, I proofread and revise myself.
I sit in your palms and am published.

I live to redesign myself.
I am a goddess made in my image.

Alone in My Head

I fumble
in the dark
of daydreams,
toppling over
running reams
of scenes
from another
time that,
most likely,
will never
come again.

Alone in
my head
I
fall outta
the present,
lost
like a
traveler at
a fork--
asking how?
When did
the road end?

It's safer
in here.
I tell
myself
lies
to keep
from losing
memories
gone like
puffs of wind.

when will
the light
open the
door, raise
a window,
permit me
to see
she's gone,
not coming
back for
me?

Alone in
this place
I will
crawl
to the
stairwell,
feel, touch,
sweet talk
the switch
that illuminates
the passage to
my heart of darkness.

There---
Love
floods
me
baptizes
me
in
self-adoration.
I
bloom
finally.

Behind the Facade

You exist
Stitched in your soul's embroidery
Where we are laced   in a skin-tight weave
That recognizes no beginning
Respects no end
A silent pattern that screams   US   breathed into your Flesh
Your imprint   s e n d s   me   after my
breath
Each time you unfurl tenderness like air-dried kisses
Embossed on the wisps of your tassels' fringes

I know
The hyperbole you wear when the front door closes   its
        respectability
A public image projected to air the planned program
You televise   your posturing
Beyond reproach beyond circumspect
Your hidden tapestry an artifice of our love
Chain mailed against the inevitable brick you perceive

        S   h   a   T   T   e   r   I   n   g

The fragile glass of a shadowbox displaying our inscrutable passion
Like art
To be shielded from soiled stares and ill impressions

I am
The outward show   of Myself
And as such I dust the layers of doom and scatter clouds of
gloom in my haste to dismiss pretence
Like a lover finally turned outdoors, sullen and blue, and though untrue

Begging to stay to get it right to stand in the Light
Behind the façade
I reach for the charade folded neatly
In the cherry wood shadowbox
Whose glass splinters like diamond chips across the hardwood
Your hammer my skeleton key

I cradle your precious veneer all the way to the porch
Where it streams out before me in waves of colors
An affectation of a rainbow
Under whose arch at whose end, I face the front

I pound a deep-seated sham from your heirloom
That hugs the banister for dear life
As it releases the trimmings of what the neighbors
Have gone near-sighted to witness for years

Before you can question your nudity flying like a flag liberated
In the softly saluting April breeze
My hands explain lifting your breastplate
While my lips elaborate kissing your chakras

                    F   R   E   E

I love me   I love you   I love them   I love us   I
love Love

In the Madam bedroom, I closet your façade against the odds of losing
you

Blood Ties

Under fluttering colorful hijabs,
You stare out of faces
That mirror
Mine
High foreheads
Dark skins
Wide mouths
Your coily, sometimes wavy hair
African beauty quietly queenly
Tying
Us to the Continent.

When I cover,
We are birds of paradise
On parade
Draped in flowing veils and flashing scarves and loud body
wraps,
Our faces reminiscent of people and lands
Across
The sea and
Street.

Unveiled,
I greet your curiosity
At my head
Uncovered
Wild, locked, and unrelentingly free.

Yesterday,
I wondered about
The veil you wore
Like invisible queens

Demure in your sovereignty
Amongst this urban plurality.
Were you

Destined to be
A shawled outline
Of second-class citizenry?

Your steps reticent, serene
Afraid to be openly heard?

A public anomaly, a glitch in
Sexuality?

Today,
I know not intuitively
And I emulate you.
Perhaps your unassuming royalty
Invites me to don the
Hijab
Under which I'm
Connected by face, blood, peace, grace, and reign.
Our blood ties
Bind us in a
Cornucopia
Of ways
I have not yet
Begun
To contemplate.

Dead-end Streets

Dead-end streets lead nowhere
No how
Like empty relationships that refuse to die
The holdin' on
Driving you insane
Because you know
Intuitively
Empirically
What somehow
Oughta be plain
Before her eyes.
But street signs aren't easily seen in the dark
So
Bruised emotions gotta be handled with care
While
Desire drives itself
Toward destinations
YOU
Don't care to go.

I Watched a Leaf Fall

There was no struggle,
No fight,
Not even a protest
Against January's might.
There was no petition to thwart her frosty rain or
Proclamation to sustain another day.
There was only a slight fluttering in the falling away.
Chariot awaiting, Leaf released her long
Love affair with Limb
And rode a limber breeze
To Ground's fertile embrace,
While I espied the skies through my kitchen window
As I peacefully rocked *mi nieto,*
Hazel eyes affably bowing to Sleep.
Both sweet deeds left me intrigued
At Mama Nature's wordless ease
Of showing us how to navigate the maze of our days,
Segueing from one calm dignity into another,
The rendezvous better and better,
Minus the demand to control another
Or command a situation out of our hands.
It was all there in the falling of a leaf today.

you have not taught me fear

i bow to no one
especially no one perfectin'
the antics you thought had me done

don't you yet hear the resouNDDDDin' ssssssslam
of the closin' door?

baby, you don't live here no more

i am a tigress on the limb
no, there is nothin' you can say to
make your entry back in

flowers?
leave them on my stoop
love letter?
send it via the net
that's not my concern I haven't
opened the last one yet

i'm not frightened of the walkin' away
and don't think the way you lay the pipe is yo' ticket to stay
ladies already lined up to play
with the goddess you took for granted
like the door don't swing both ways

can we say
i don't just relish the heat
in the fire   amongst the embers   i like to be tweaked
sweet pea

you're a busy street I aim to cross
and since i'm used to gettin' on with my life
like mary j., i don't need no mo' strife

when the brocade curtain hits the stage
i ain't dazed
the sidewalk might seem undeniably safe
but, baby, the action in the street
gives me leeway to meet
her
standin' on this curb watchin' you watch me

nope, you ain't taught me to fear

i got faith from here to here
facin' the crowd, i stand proud
i step on the crack and
roll-on when you turn back

don't matter she ain't here yet
i'll speak her into my arms
cause cryin' the blues
ain't somethin' i often do
that's too much time i don't intend to lose

i got plans, darlin'
and they don't include you
you had yo' chance and
blew it, too

Resurrections

I have known tombs
Dark, cavernous, water-deprived, silent
Tombs. I have buried my soul
Deep within these tombs.

But I have had enough of tombs,
Thus, I resurrect myself,
Rolling the rock away from once-padded doors
like Jesus calling
Lazarus forth.

Looking back,
I realize the cocoon
Of locked rooms
Is a crouching dragon
Behind layers
Of me.

I will be visible
Loved trusted esteemed caressed, yes.
So when I look in the mirror
I'll greet the trinity of
Me, myself and I---
The Ubiquitous Us.
I bow not to the twin gnomes, Abuse and Lies.
Behind the veil of
Self-trust, I rise.

The layers of others' approval
I peel away in
Peals of self-loving laughter.
In the rear of one tomb, I

Reach back for my Little Girl's
Hand
Pet her cheeks
And brush neglect from her
Dress.
I embrace her, walk her to the Light.
Outside our room
I kneel before her scuffed
Cardboard-filled shoes.

Confused, she squints
Rubs memory from her
Eyes
Watery with scenes of
Being pushed aside
Looked over
Passed down
Given up
Left behind.

I teach her not to blame.
I teach her to cheerlead self.
I teach her every goal is within her reach.

"Don't run,"
I tell her.
"When you are shown love, walk.
Don't deny yourself, my dove, you
Deserve manna pouring
From the sky,
For there will be those
Who try
To sabotage your joy.
Push the boulder of faith

Uphill
Knowing you mistreat
Yourself
When you demand from others
What they cannot
Give."

Little Girl understood,
Sat upon the rock
Beside me
While we soaked in
The sunset,
Resurrected us two,
Embracing
The
Love
Of
Self
We
Never
Knew.

Bitch, Be Busy

She hasn't called this New Year.

For that, I ought to rejoice

And thank the Goddess

I don't have to

Remind me to

"Bitch, be busy."

But, I know like she knows

That if she calls

I **will** answer.

It's a tacit understanding I never

Had to say.

She's got it that way.

Since I wrote her goodbye poem last month

Since I love her here or gone,

I pacify myself

Like this, "Bitch be busy,"

Moving on.

A Fantasy Revisited

i regret the night i ever
rode you into that
scheming wind
the ride a drip of
cum-dipped days
sticky with a
flava i've yet
to Listerine
from my bitter tongue
your aftertaste
based with
meth-laced
fabrications that
rankle my
heart even now

but that soprano sky
was an eiderdown
blanket
against
our entwined thighs and
the crescendo
of moonbeams wily
how
was
i
to
disown
moans
of
spoiled honey

Abduction Poem

Even before I know it
My pen has planned your
Abduction

Through the lines
Of this poem
The ripe aroma
Of my thoughts
Waft
Between and through
Up and around
These words
Alerting you
To the passion
That could be ours
If you came
Close enough
To sniff
The scratch-off
Label

Do you smell
The hijack
Coming?
You should
I'm running
Game so
Smooth
So insane
My kiss and fastest
Planes will
Render you
Permanently disabled
You'll be
The Most Satisfied

Prisoner
When the key is
Turned
The sound of
Capture
Revealing
Secrets
Guarded
Like
Fort Knox
On lock

Be my hostage, Babee,
Come
Unbuckle Uncle Sam's
War games
Take a chance
Play for a change
Follow the
Reconnaissance
I run
Down
Under
Don't
Worry,
My Love,
Believe
I won't leave
I'll hold you
After
The thunder
Step outta
That uniform
Let me slip it on
Never mind the boots
Though the contrast of you
And regulation

Wreaks my intent
'Cause I wanna leave you
Spent
But now I'm
inked
my pen rent
Bent
On handcuffing
A view that
Threatens my shoot
My skyjack
Me calling for back-up
'Cause I'm doing
This

Halt! That's an order!
I control this border.

I am D O I N G ttthhhiiisss, soldier!

Black lace and
Heels under fatigues
Inspect me
Now
Ask me how
I'll confiscate
Your take-down
Removing the thinking:
You can't be strong
Looking up
Back flat
Abducted
White flag
Flying
Breath caught
Trying
To hand glide

The current
That floats you
To this Four-Star Commander
On whose page
In whose poem
Under whose pen
You recline
Dripping sweat
All other duties annexed
Until the next time
I write our foreplay.

Bondage

What I know is
I don't know
Anything
About bondage
Though submission
Directs me when you are
Present.

I cannot look full upon you.
You are a heat source
A meteor.
Instead, I want to lie under you
Feel the intensity of your heat
Take the moon rock you
Thrust into my crater.

Where are your chains?   You know
The ones that wrapped themselves about
My heart the August evening
I first saw you
At a backyard barbecue
A beer
Caught in your grip
Where I longed to be
Chained like keys to your hip.
You are my love letter
Evoking pink sighs and fuchsia moans
Culled from
Surrender.
The touch of your hand
On the small of my back
Creates an arch
That locks me in position:
Your preferred view.

Welcome to "The Valley of the Siren."
Here. This is the key
To your every fantasy.
I'll resist nothing
Propose you do
What you will.
I consent
I acquiesce
Until you are supine between my thighs.

No. I know nothing
Of S&M games
Or why someone would want
To be subdued.
But when you are near
Or your name creeps into
My space,
Scenes take shape:
Arrayed in black vinyl
Soft as leather
I slip to my knees
Bow my head
Patiently awaiting
The jewelry that is your choke chain.
In deference
I listen for your command
Compliance, I understand, in
Black stilettos
Poised to dance   strut
A Fem Manifesto
I am the answer to any question
You conjure.
Black lace at my breasts,
Crotch-less clit bejeweled.
My wrists you tie in haste.
You can't wait.
You brand me with your breath
Lock the door and

Toss the key to the floor.
And I whimper
While you watch me hang from the ceiling
My flesh pressed against thick nylon.
I am balled, exposed, no entries barred
Delirious for your pleasure.

Bound, I am your limo ride
And your driver.
Wrists cuffed in pink fluff
Ankles clasped together
In licorice
Edible undies sticky---
I will leave a masterpiece
Of hickies
Across the terrain
Of your plains.
From you,
I will bring punany rains
To rival
The monsoons of India
The Philippines
And Burma.
When our scenes dissolve in climax, I will leave these stilettos
My handcuffs
For your senses to behold
Until you return
To demand that climatic mix of capitulation
And adulation
The reasons why you came.
O the sweetness of Love's exchange.

Got Pussy?

Rides high across her breasts
       arresting my gaze
       before I clock her other
       assets.
I pray to breathe static air
       as she passes,
       her "Hey, Lady" lightening striking in my
       "Hey Yourself" glances
Yes, her effect, she knows is doing it
       got me knowing she's got it
       while I'm imaginin' we do it
       for Sapphic, Kama Sutra-choreographed poses.

Her presence fills the room
       oblivious to male amazement
       some women mesmerized, too.
There is little compliant
       about a woman who saunters into a space
       confident in her dykedom,
       no apologies to make.
Her query in active voice
       is anything but dreary on a Monday dressed out in
uniform gray.
The question boasts
       a woman too bold to be deleted
       under twice-flicked stares
       and "What the hell does that say?" flares.

Unobtrusive
       she isn't.
What she wants is what she gets
       despite whose eyes perplex, digesting…

What makes her tick
Strikes fire under her stick
Makes her want to lick
Pass dead presidents
and settle down to circumvent
Bachelorette Boulevard
For a home
On Love's Lane,
     'cause when Cupid strikes,
     it's all the same.

***

So I catch her eye
     answer with a smile,
     since I love a dyke with style and something to say,
     my own T's message on esplanade:

"100% Woman Lover:
Keep Pussy…Always."

Then I percolate with the countless, stimulating ways
     I can give her what she's askin',
     though it might take a lifetime to put it to her straight,
     'cause I can put it down on the back porch
     in the sun or in the shade
     while serving up skinny glasses of chilled lemonade,
     my gourmet cookies crumbled from the bottom step to
her Escalade.

We can do it in the attic in a pool of afternoon sun or better yet
     on top of the roof where the leak don't run.
It's on and poppin, Ma, and you set to have big fun
     when I hang off the drainpipes,

my senses on lit,
me babblin' my ecstasy, gasping till she says, "Quit,"
like I wish I would ask her to desist if I could move my lips.
But she hasn't seen anything yet. I can roll that sweet thang out
so wet
      she simply forgets
      everything outside of ripe raspberries and black cherries
      in the heat of summer with nothing wrapped around her
May pole
      but my legs hugging her ass, my knees stuck to her
      stomach.
Excuse us, honey, while we wipe the traces of our desire.

I Come Out

Softly,
Each time I see her
Realizing I've lived four decades
To sit in her presence and
Lose my thoughts gazing into her smoldering eyes.
A blank expression muffles my words,
Which float like ash across our candlelit table.
I am silenced.
Then miraculously, she reaches out and saves me,
Screwing up her nose and poking her fingers into her cheeks
Causing me to erupt in medicinal laughter, unabashed and free.
She heals me under her volcanic balm.

I come out...

Melodiously,
In the most unexpected places,
In some unusual faces
Like the one that can't seem to understand
Nor care
That I'm not charmed;
No alarms
Blaring when he grins and tells me the many ways
His dick can touch my skin.
Machismo won't let him begin
To disconnect without my number before "The End."
I don't brawl   I simply say,
"My friend, I ask but one question tonight,
'Is it detachable?'
If so, it might be alright."
Baffled, he comprehends by degrees,
And I continue as sweet as you please:

"I'm sure all your dick exploits are commendable,
But it'd be irreprehensible
For you to top my Beautiful Butch's incomprehensible
Delectable
Biodegradable
Insatiable
Dickaliciously unquenchable
Dick deeds.
I don't have time to relay the awards and honors
Conferred on her dick,
A charter dick, its title deed known far and wide,
For pleasing and being leased
Only to me,
But if you want to know about detachable dicks,
Visit the Dick Hall of Fame
There her name and picture and dicks are framed.
So goodbye and do call again."

I do it organically. Come out, that is, sensually,

Yes, dramatically,
When I enter a space
Beside a smoothly gliding   almost sliding
Woman who rivals the notion masculinity
Can't be redefined like the notes on a musical scale
Dancing in snake-skin shoes
And expensive tie and tails.
Her sheet music makes me sing
An aria
In
Soprano
And bass
All over this place
In my attempt to tell the world:

How amazing her fingers play me
How her tongue masters my reeds

How her arms shield me
How her mind makes me throb with harmony.

Won't someone halt the conductor
While I moan the chorus for this tune?

I come out...

Gracefully
Like stars tossed up and scattered
Against a canopy of bars
O Goddess
Let me come out hard
Pressed, that is, against her
Woman's terrain
As my feet seek her legs and thighs
Like the morning glory vine hugs the
Wood it climbs in the light of a
New November morning
My hydroponic heart
beats the bars of my adoration
My flesh no longer needed
To protect its fragile
Heart notes
Exposed   naked and free

I Wanna Fuck You But...

I don't wanna stay.
I just wanna love you when I'm ready to play.
I make no promises, but you won't complain.
You look so sweet; I don't wanna ever see you in pain.

I wanna fuck you, but you must understand.
You're special. I don't just ask for everybody's hand.
I wanna fuck *you*, make *you* moan, make *you* sigh.
I wanna take your kisses in the softest drive-by.

Baby, you haven't known true fucking.
I can see it in your look. Stop ducking!
Me? I can look your knees weak.
My voice alone can render you unable to speak.

C'mere. Lay by my side.
I'm gonna kiss you until your fear subsides.
Then I'll stroke you where it aches,
Make you shiver like you're standing in a freezing lake.

I wanna fuck you, but all keys I must possess.
None of you will be off-limits when you I undress.
How else will I know how to fuck you best?
Baby, believe me when I confess, I'm unlike the rest.

I wanna fuck you any way I choose...
In the park, in my car, you can't lose.
I got climaxes for you alone.
I know a thousand and one ways to own your moans.
Angel, I wanna fuck you, but you gotta give it to me willing.
You're not a fuck thing, and I don't do stealing.
When I touch your knees, I want your juices coming down.

Love's perfume outta be rising high, swirling round and round.
I want you on your knees,
Begging, "Please, baby, please."
You know you wanna be fucked, but you also wanna relationship.
I say, "We are relating. Ours is the ultimate companionship."

And on those occasions when I wanna be fucked,
I want you to give it up; I wanna feel sufficiently sucked.
I want you to spread yourself across me like jam on toast.
I want to sizzle and sputter, like a well-basted roast.

Let me say again, I do not boast.
I will stretch your legs from coast to coast.
When you take your next breath to breathe,
You will murmur my name and pray I'm back before I leave.

So what's the deal? Exercise your own will.

Speak your mind.
Leave other people's opinions behind.
Remember, if Society had her way,
You'd be single and lonely or married and on layaway.

I wanna fuck you.
But you gotta wanna play.
And if not now, I'll see you next time around.
Maybe then you'll be ready to get on down.

I Wanna Love You But...

...You're a Fortune 500 Dynamo
Running her own show
Got corporate respect and powerful exec's listed on her Rolodex
Yet you wouldn't know how to love if your Dream Woman
Appeared with a note from Jesus, reading,
"I don't raise hell. Let me love you for a spell."
You'd giggle, call ya gyrl,
Describe some fool think she can fit in your world.

I wanna love you
But...
You got a fixation on staying fucked up. Don't you know when
enough's enough?
How can you listen to yourself
To know yourself
If every time your Angels speak
They have to let it go
Wait till the effects of the smoke recede
So you can see?

Gyrl, it's true. You hearing it from me, Boo.
I wanna love you but
...you never have shit to say
When you've got my undivided attention,
Yet when it's my turn
You flipping summersaults
Tripping and dipping
Carrying on like I'm forever disrespecting
Your right to say
Whatever you can't get out
When I can't stay.
I really do wanna love you but...

You ain't going to treat me like you did ya last gyrl
Kicking in her door and unleashing verbal theatrics on her
Living room floor.
I am a gentlewoman.
I rather make love half the night
And spend the other half whispering love poems
To make whatever ails you right.

Listen, I just wanna love you
Until you clearly grasp
I could be a compound no other woman can scale.
I'd surround you with a love, if imprisoned, would need no bail.
No sacrifice too large, no surrender too small
I'd give you my all,
But you blame me for your hurts
And expend too much time keeping up dirt.
Actually, I tired of wanting to love you.
I'm learning life isn't hard.
Just people's perceptions, thus I did wanna love you, sweetie,
A moment ago. Now I take back my desire
As I let you go, 'cause I will myself not to want you no mo'.

I'll remember instead to love me like I need to be loved
And that does not include you and the whack way you love
So forget my name, erase my numbers from your phones
And get a pet for the time you'll have when you're alone.
The passion has passed, my precious, so click...I'm not at home.

Love Profiles Monogamy: An 8-word story poem

Feet meet,

Make six.

Triad complete.

Throuple bubble.

Many Rains Ago

across a wind-tossed sea

back against sand and scant shrubbery

in a Motherland

my soul still sees

I lay me down, head wrap undone near a sack of date palms

fabric pooled at your ankles jeweled

the kissing wind abloom with acacia and tamarind,

we flowered at high noon, our oasis love unseen.

You Are the Sun

rising inside me

me, your Leaning Tower

you, shattering my solitude

daring me to run

from intrusively sweet

messages

texted throughout the hours

persistent links

cuffing my attention

Is it possible? Is it right?

From a parallel galaxy

you burn through my nights

I hover over delete

the memory of meeting you in my dreams

no one will believe

It's just too much to confide

To anyone

so I hide

then wait for you to find me at sunrise

or anytime I close my eyes

Unvanquished

I AM

through the storm and the pain

the wind and the rain

the memories and the former taint.

Though circumstances sometimes rise up

funnel and uproot

buckle and pollute my terrain,

my inner me remains

beautifully

unscathed.

*

Yes, it's true…whatever you've

heard. I've been raped

sexually abused

misused

held down

discounted.

Despite bad, sad things looming

like terrorizing trolls on

a bridge,

I can never be

diminished.

I'm the grace of those

who came before me,

a prototype

for those

coming after me.

*

Read the memo. I AM more than a lover.

I'm a conqueror

conquering the wilderness

of self.

I buoy me.

In regal robes, I

wrap these gentle, stalwart

shoulders

in the warmth

that no one or nothing

mars the stroke

of the spiritual brush

that paints me

ME.

Squelch my beauty. No such

tomfoolery.

*

Look. I AM an explorer

discovering new regions

within myself.

Still standing, I

don't mind

others knowing

where I've been.

The gem is in

where I'm going.

Not hiding

beyond quaking

only celebrating

any idiosyncrasy

you might discover

about me.

See, I L O V E me

in all of who

I AM.

There are no regrets.

Where I've been

makes for the best of me.

I AM

Methuselah, a bristlecone pine,

my branches lifted to the skies

for over 5,000 years.

Believe me. You

and what army

gonna dull my shine?

I AM

deeper than a Faulkner novel,

Yoknapatawpha County at a loss to

tell my story.

*

Unsullied

I reflect on the roads

I've known,

roads like detours

filled with years of

interred silence.

But they couldn't traffic me.

At the crossroads, I realized

I was still here:

the anchor beneath my ship

the sass and sexy in the wiggle in my hips.

You see the glint in my gaze?

I own the sensual and sexy all up in this place.

Rape, you will never define me.

Abuse, be my stepping stone

on my victorious climb towards

my Greater Good

on this magnanimous journey.

Somewhere

In my lifetime
Unlike those about which Hyman sang
I wish I had kissed your lips
Lips that I once wished away
Lips that persisted in my days
calling me out of night sweats
Your words sliding under my IG posts
Conversational...thoughtful...gallant
In a voice I've only heard in your posts

I peruse you
In Facebook moments
Wanting you to brush up against me
Like I want to brush up against you
You, somewhere smelling good under thick locs
Just so much forbidden fruit
Our lips separated by years, fears, and life's situations

But somewhere
I hold you tight
To still this beating heart
Driving me
To wade through
Move around gossip
Sweep it under Qigong's mudras or
Gentle hands
My chi discounting the
"No, it's not right"
Notions in my head
Though, sometimes I'm brave and
We tumble back into my dreams
And love our way across other landscapes
Surviving plagues and ages
When our ages, stations, and occupations
Are incontestable
No fucks dispensed

Somewhere
In this lifetime
I will inhale your scent
Embrace you with fierce intent
Me drenched
In vibes of your 80's musical sense
Of what it will mean to be
You and me
Lyrically
Sans past or future
Forever in the omnipotent present
Ready to be undressed
Stripped of judgment
Glazed in sweat
The one Marvin advised
We wake up to
Morning, noon, or night
On our way to
Making love right

I Knew You in Other Lives

We were poets
Who welded pens sharper than swords
We were overlords
of peace and harmony
pulverizing the notion of might over right

Through the ages
I was your fortress, and you were my wife
Then you were my child
I your isle of safe space
Once we took the forces of evil
Compressed them into storm clouds that
Watered the land, then we
Demanded Power trade places with the Everyman

We'd run with spears and gallop our steeds into battles
We'd already won
The feel of the victory therapeutic
Had us drifting on mushroom vibes
After we poked the pupils out of a Cyclops' eyes
And walked with Hera through Roman streets
We knew not defeat

For us, Cleopatra dismissed Mark Anthony
A royal triad, we drove the reigning class mad
The pyramids were our playground and
Rippling time, we invited Queen Nzinga, Oshun, Oya
Yemoja and Mami Wata to goddess galas where
We bathed their feet and regaled them with mental
Feasts

I knew you when you blew Freedom like smoke
Into the eyes of buckra
Had them running amuck
On their way to the bellies of cargo jets
Their destiny, a free flight to Africa to experience
The wisdom of the Dahomey Amazons

And yes, you've known me
Since Time began
I took fire in the palm of my hands
Hurled suns into distant galaxies
And you looked implosions into spinning comets
To thwart cosmic tragedies
For the wonderment of astronomers and anyone with
Eyes to see
Together, we made magic and called it fantasy

For Requaya

You Cannot Pass This Way

No matter what path you take,
Unloved.
Whether
Joe A. Shmoe, Betty Boo, or From Nowhere Nancy,
Someone fancies you,
Here and on High.

We are celestial,
Waiting to
Recognize
Ourselves
And rise
Higher
In thought, deed, belief, circumstances,
And Love.

Thus, be blessed.
Create.
Make love.
Share.
And dare.

About the Author

CLAUDIA MOSS is a poet, fiction writer, and YouTuber. She is the author of two novels: **Dolly: The Memories of a High School Graduate** and **If You Love Me**, **Come**, and the coming novel, **Not Without Passion**. **Soft Tsunami i**s her first poetry collection.

www.ingramcontent.com/pod-product-compliance
Lightning Source LLC
Chambersburg PA
CBHW060940120626
46557CB00003B/1072

* 9 7 8 0 9 8 3 2 6 9 7 1 7 *